MY FRIEND IS HIV POSITIVE

BASED ON REAL LIFE STORIES

RAJAN CHAWLA

Copyright © Rajan Chawla
All Rights Reserved.

This book has been published with all efforts taken to make the material error-free after the consent of the author. However, the author and the publisher do not assume and hereby disclaim any liability to any party for any loss, damage, or disruption caused by errors or omissions, whether such errors or omissions result from negligence, accident, or any other cause.

While every effort has been made to avoid any mistake or omission, this publication is being sold on the condition and understanding that neither the author nor the publishers or printers would be liable in any manner to any person by reason of any mistake or omission in this publication or for any action taken or omitted to be taken or advice rendered or accepted on the basis of this work. For any defect in printing or binding the publishers will be liable only to replace the defective copy by another copy of this work then available.

Contents

Preface

Sometimes, something happens in your life that completely changes the way you used to look at it. Either you meet someone, read something, listen to someone, follow someone, or get influenced by someone, that introduces you with the mind-blowing realities of the life. My main objective of writing this book is to reiterate that life is like a game of adventure. We just have to face every phase of it which comes with different challenge, with the aim of winning.

In this book, an attempt has been made to present the personal stories of people living with HIV in an inspirational form. Although all these stories are based on true events, the names of all the characters in this book have been changed along with the related places and events to preserve the privacy of the real-life characters. This has been done because the absence of information and awareness combined with old-fashioned beliefs lead people to fear getting HIV. Additionally, many people think of HIV as a disease that only certain groups and people get. This leads to negative value judgements about people who are HIV Infected. These people face discrimination, losing social status and role, changes in the patterns of relationships (intimacy), losing jobs and financial resources. Above all their families abandon them too. These stories are of those brave people who faced HIV with full courage by breaking the shackles of frustration and despair and today they are happily living their lives.

~ *Rajan Chawla*

• • •

Acknowledgements

I have read a lot of stories of people facing challenges in life and fighting them hard. But listening those stories from the real-life characters and meeting them in person was a thrilling and inspiring life experience. I thank all those people who shared their life secrets with me and allowed me to pen down their stories here in this book.

I hope readers will not only get the inspiration from these stories but an inner strength too to fight the challenges in their life.

~Rajan Chawla

• • •

CHAPTER I

This Problem Has No Solution!

My phone rings......

'Hello!'

'Hello Rajan...!'

'Yeah, tell me Rahul'

'I feel like giving up my life'

'What!'

'Yeah, I no longer want to live'

'Have you gone crazy? What happened!! Tell me if there's a problem, there must be a solution for it too.'

'No, this problem has no solution'

'Please listen to me, don't do anything stupid, think of your mother, Rahul. I'm your friend and we can discuss the issue and find the solution together'

'No, you are not understanding'

Thank God Rahul lives nearby and while talking to him over phone I reached his home. Without saying hello to his mother who was cooking dinner, I straight away rushed to his room.

'What is this, Rahul?' Are you nuts? Why are you behaving like this? What happened?'

'Rajan – I am Positive'

'What!!?? But why are you talking so negative?'

'I have got tested positive for HIV'

Five seconds' pin drop silence with eyes wide opened.... (back ground music – La*** Lag gaye.mp3)

'I always told you to use protection, but when have you listened to anyone...*feel nahi aati, feel nahi aati, ab le le feel bh******! ('condoms take a toll on my pleasure', now feel the* *pleasure of HIV, you sis** f**)*

'Even though you have condom in your wallet, you don't take it out, how can you be so f****g careless and irresponsible, Rahul'

Rahul was sitting on the chair with his head down.

'Have you double checked the report?', Show me the report...'

Rahul said he got the test done in two different private labs (with fake names) and the results are same. With tears in his eyes, he asked me' What should I do now'? Should I die?

'How would I know, I don't have any idea about this shit, man!! And I sat on the adjacent chair.

'Ok wait a minute, I have a friend in NGO and they work for HIV awareness etc. Let me call him and ask what should be done and I'm sure there would be the solution to this problem too. But you promise that you will not take any wrong step that you and all of us will have to repent later'

'Rahuuuuuullllll, Dinner is ready son, come' Rahul's mother called.

• • •

CHAPTER II

Rahul – The Heartthrob

With Adonis-like physique, Rahul has sparkling personality. Not only he has a muscular body but his washboard abs are only too hot to handle for any girl. His school and then college friends were jealous of him as all the girls were crazy about Rahul and no girl used to give chance to any other guy. He is the heart-throb of the town.

He is okay in the studies and wants to have a career in modelling and Film Industry. He goes to gym regularly, posts his videos on social media and he has got thousands of followers, mostly girls and even guys.

He is a straight guy but most of the time he gets messages from boys. He sometimes shows those messages to me and laughs like anything. He takes life very easy. He is a person living in today and does not worry about tomorrow. He never plans anything. He is the guy who goes with the flow.

• • •

CHAPTER III

Spilling The Beans

One of my friends Saurabh who works for an NGO counselled Rahul and asked him to get himself tested again from the government hospital. He assured all the help and guidance.

Rahul was scared as hell and he was not speaking at all. I was with him and asking the questions on his behalf. Saurabh said" If you're infected by HIV that doesn't mean the life is going to end. HIV Infected people can lead a healthy life for a long time with proper medical care".

He explained the ART Treatment - Anti-retroviral therapy (ART), if taken timely and regularly, suppresses replication effectively. He assured that proper counselling will be done at the hospital.

The whole process of testing and results are kept confidential. In government hospitals, testing, medicines and counselling is free of cost and the data is kept private too. Rahul was initially skeptical about revealing his secret to Saurabh, but the way Saurabh not only explained the whole thing with great calmness but also gave him a confidence and hope, Rahul was impressed by him. It seemed that fear was starting to subside from Rahul's mind. Saurabh said that we could trust on him for all the confidentiality as he and his NGO help people who are HIV positive in guiding them and encouraging them to start their treatment as soon as possible, stick to the treatment and live a healthy life ahead.

• • •

CHAPTER IV

A Day Of Embarrassments

What strikes your mind when you hear the term 'Government Hospital'? Crowds, long queues, people sitting on floors moaning in pain, patients of the relatives wandering here and there, seems to be a very pessimistic and a super sad place. And above all the question of cleanliness and hygiene raises the eyebrows. Looking at the employees there, it seems as if they are bored of doing the monotonous work every day and there is no emotion in anyone's heart.

Taking the responsibility of a good and true friend, I accompanied Rahul to get his blood test done in one of such government hospitals. Saurabh met us there and he was now taking us to the HIV lab. We both covered our faces with masks to hide our identities.

In the next moment, I saw Rahul was in the queue and Saurabh was talking to a staff member, as he might know him already. Rahul even with his mask was looking like a model and everybody was staring at him. The strange looks of the staff personnel taking details for the test, was making Rahul very uncomfortable. Saurabh then intervened,

"Are Sir ji, details lijiye na, test karwana hai, der ho rahi hai" (Please take the details, we're getting late for test)

Ignoring Saurabh, the staff came a little closer to Rahul and said "you are educated, you look like a hero, how did this happen to you?"

"Sir we have come for the blood test to confirm whether it has happened or not" Saurabh interrupted

Staff gave an annoying look to Saurabh and started taking the details from Rahul.

I could see that Rahul was not liking all of this and he wanted to run away, but I was surprised to see how patiently he was sitting and moving from one queue to another, one staff to other, like an innocent kid to get his blood test done.

After they took his blood, the lab assistant said "Reports will come by 2PM tomorrow".

There ended the embarrassments of the day!

• • •

CHAPTER V

The Result Day

Just as the heart starts beating loudly before the result of any examination, similarly riding pillion on Rahul's bike, the sound of our heart beats was coming louder than the horn.

Even after getting results from two private labs, I don't know why were we expecting miracles from the government lab. Keeping my fingers crossed, we parked the bike and there appeared the NGO worker, Saurabh.

We were at the same place, infront of the same staff staring weirdly at us and then Rahul gave me a look. I know that look very well which means he wants to kill that person at the very moment. I replied back with the look of being calm down.

Saurabh: Sir, we are here for the results

Staff Uncle (looking at Rahul): What is your name again?

Rahul: Rahul...Rahul Mehra

The middle-aged man looked among all the results and then took out Rahul's result, he opened that, started shaking his head and said "Didn't I ask you yesterday, how did it happen? Results came Positive"

At this moment I was able to feel Rahul's mental anguish to the core. I was feeling so helpless that nothing was going to help Rahul even though I wanted to. Nor did I have any words to speak.

Rahul was calm. All the people present in that small room seemed to console Rahul with their sympathetic eyes. Rahul was with his head down. The staff uncle put his hand on Rahul's shoulder and said, "Son, there is nothing to panic. You are not the first, and you are not the last either.

'Tell me when and why did you first think you should get tested??'

Rahul Replied "Sir, I have done sex without condom several times, one day an uncomfortable but a strong thought came to my mind that I should get my test done. I then got it done from the private labs, twice, where it came positive"

'So multiple partners?'

'Yes' replied Rahul

'Married'

'No'

'Oh, my goodness!!! Man, even after being so educated, how do you do such irresponsible acts? Look at you, you are no less than Hrithik Roshan and how are you treating your youthfulness'

An uneasy silence

'Don't panic now, don't feel bad about what I say, I just don't like it when the youth of the country get caught in this HIV maze.' Uncle sighed and stood up

He then instructed Saurabh to take Rahul to the ART department for the registration and for further formalities. Putting his both hands over Rahul's shoulders he said "here starts the new chapter of your life, do take care of yourself. Good Luck!".

• • •

CHAPTER VI

The New Chapter Starts

The realization that we can never be cured and we have to live with 'this unwanted thing' for our lifetime, leaves an emptiness and sadness inside.

'Today, HIV-positive diagnosis is no longer as downhearted as it once was. People having HIV are living their lives to the full and in a healthy way. Though myths around this infection still persists' Saurabh enlightened while leading us towards ART registration centre with the results in our hands.

Saurabh has already got us the OPD card and I felt he was sure that results would be positive therefore he had already instructed Rahul a day before to come with his Identity /Address proof for the registration.

As soon as we entered the ART Department with our faces covered with masks, we saw lots of people there standing in the queue either to get medicines or for counselling or for regular check-ups. Saurabh explained all this.

'*Namaste Didi, kaisi hai aap!* (Hello sister, how are you!)' asked Saurabh to the lady sitting at the registration desk.

'*Arey Rahul, aaj phir se*' (Hey Rahul, You here again)

'Ji didi, ye bhaiyan hai hamare, inka registration karana tha (Yes sister, He is my brother-like, he is here for the registration)'

Rahul whispered in my ears '*Bhai ye Saurabh roz kisi na kisi ko pakad ke lata hai kya idhar*' (Bro, does this Saurabh bring people here regularly?)

I shrugged.

'Come here and have a seat' lady told Rahul

Saurabh explained Rahul that he can ask as many questions to the lady counsellor as he wants. No question is a silly question and there's nothing to be shy about. After saying this, both of us came out of that room and Rahul's registration and counselling process started which lasted for almost 30 minutes.

Sitting outside that glass cabin, I was looking at Rahul. He was asking questions and the counsellor was answering all of them. In between, I also saw a smile on his face. It felt as if Rahul was getting the answer to his every question correctly and maybe even a positive hope too.

'How was it'? I asked eagerly when he came out

'It was good and I'm less scared now' Rahul replied with a smile

'I have to meet the doctor now and he will then prescribe the medicine I think' Rahul added

After spending 15 minutes with the doctor, he came out, took the medicine which was free of cost; He told me that now he has to go through various tests within a month. Showing the box of medicine, he said that he has to take one tablet daily without a miss. And from here begins the never-ending journey of Medicines and Tests which will end only with his death. While telling this, his eyes filled with tears, but I could also see a fighting spirit visible in his eyes as if he wanted to say that whatever it is now, he would fight these situations and move forward in his life. As soon as I said this, I put my hand on his shoulder and he hugged me.

'Okay, I am done here, it is now your responsibility that you take your medicine daily and get yourself tested as and when asked for. In case you face any difficulty in any of the tasks, please feel free to reach out to me' interrupted Rahul in the emotional scene.

'Hey thanks mate for all your help, you have awakened my dying self-confidence and showed a ray of hope' said Rahul, showing gratitude to Saurabh

'It is my duty and you should say thanks to your friend Rajan' ~Saurabh replied with a smile.

• • •

CHAPTER VII

Should We Tell Mom?

A million-dollar question and the answer to this is not easy to give. What should we tell, how should we tell? It seems like trouble after trouble, tension after tension and as Rahul says it is not only the unending journey of medicine and tests but life-long embarrassment too.

And how does society treat the HIV positive people, we had experienced the live demonstration in the hospital itself.

By telling all this to his mother, Rahul did not want to increase her worries any more. But was Rahul doing the right thing? Such a big secret of his life, did he want to keep it limited only to himself and myself? Keeping courage, I adviced him that it would be right thing if he would tell his mother. This would not only lighten the burden of his heart but his mother would be able to take good care of him.

As usual he ignored my suggestion and said that this was not the right time to disclose such a big news to his mother. In future, if he would feel sharing, he would do so accordingly.

I didn't feel appropriate to argue with him or explain to him at that point of time. I gave a simple nod and left.

• • •

CHAPTER VIII

Touch Only Spreads Love

Fear impairs your ability to think. It removes intellectual cells in your brain and establishes its own bacteria. Because of that you start thinking illogically.

I was with an HIV infected person for the whole day, after that I was in the hospital among the same people. Somehow, I started feeling strange. I took a bath; had a proper meal and then with a cup of hot tea in my hand, I was now on my study table. I don't know how I was feeling as if something had happened to me, both physically and mentally? Perhaps there was an overdose of both fatigue and stress.

A whatsapp notification flashed on my mobile. It was from Saurabh and that was just what I needed perhaps at that time.

"Don't you worry, *Choone se sirf pyar phailta hai*" (Touch only spreads love) concatenated with a winking emoji.

'Yeah Yeah' I replied with the same emoji.

Another text received from Rahul

'Will pick you at 7'o clock tomorrow'

'Wait...for what and to where!!'

'To the hospital again, for the more tests they asked for'

'F**** NO!!'

'F**** with Condom this time and YES, be ready...Bye'

'Had this condom been used earlier, situation would have been different today'

'☹'

Ever since Rahul's secret got out to me, 'L*** Lag gaye.mp3' kept ringing in my ears.
Good Night Rajan!

• • •

CHAPTER IX

Life's More Colors Than Rainbow – Ajay's story

Now accompanying Rahul to the hospital, whether to take medicines or get any test done, had become a part of my quarterly to-do list. While waiting for Rahul, I started talking to the people sitting there, listening to their stories, knowing them.

That one day, I was sitting on the bench and checking my mobile, then a voice fell in my ear

'*bhaiya aap bhi yaha apni dawai lene aaye ho*' (Brother, have you also come here to get your medicine?)

'No No, I am fine, I am here with someone' I replied to that teenager

'How come you're here'?

'I'm here to get my medicines, I'm infected no…HIV'

I was literally shocked that how come a cute looking young teenage guy of that young age be infected by HIV.

'*Naam kya hai tumhara*' (What's your name?)

'*Ajay*'

'*ye kaise hua tumhe?*' (How did this happen to you?)

'*Papa ko tha, fir unse mummy ko aur dono se mujh ko hua;* (My father got infected first, my mother got from him, finally transferred to me)

'*HIV ke sath hi paida hua mein*' (I'm born with HIV) told Ajay with a smile

That boggled my mind literally. I was shocked to the core that I didn't know what to say to him.

'*kya hua bhaiya, kuch bole nahi aap*' (what happened brother, you didn't say anything) boy asked with a smile

'*main kya kahu? Bina kasoor ke tumhe Zindagi ne saza di*' (What shall I say? Life punished you without any fault)

'*ha ha ha, zindagi ke indradhanush se jyada rang hai bhaiya, sab apni kismat pehle se hi likhwa ke aate hai*'

(Life has more colors than rainbow, everyone comes to get their luck already written)

'How did you manage now with all this'

'My mom is dead now; my dad is ill, I live with my grandmother and elder sister'

'Oh is she too...?'

'No no, she is safe'

'I study in a school, come here in the hospital every three months when my medicines are over'

'What about the income source'

'My grandmother's and father's pension'

'So, your relatives know about this?'

'Yes, and neither they visit our home, nor they want our cousins to play with me'

'What about your class mates'

'Only my best friend knows, else they (school administration) would have expelled me out'

'So, you don't feel bad about all this, about the life you are living'

'Initially, when I came to know about all this and I started to understand, then I felt very bad, I also got angry, but now it has become a part of my life, then why shouldn't I try to live my life as happily as possible? **Every living day is a win for me.**'

'Amazing spirit you have; keep that high always, there are lots who can learn from you, my dear friend'

'Thank you *bhaiya* (brother), I should go, they have called up my name'

'Yeah, good luck Ajay!'

He smiled.

What a great inspiring lesson, the young kid had taught to me. From that day I decided that I would come with Rahul to the hospital and meet people and listen to their inspiring stories.

In a way thanks to Rahul that I got to see the others colors of life than Rainbow.

• • •

CHAPTER X

What's Left In The Life To Hide – Sujata's Story

Generally, the hospital staff comes to work at 9 AM, but people start queuing up from 7 AM itself. As they come, they put their cards on the closed window itself. When the staff personnel arrives at 9 o'clock, they look at the cards one by one.

'Sujata'

'Yes ma'am'

'Your application has been approved' with a big smile on her face, Staff aunty told Sujata who was first in the queue

'Thank You ma'am' Nirmala expressed gratitude

Two ladies started congratulating Sujata. Rahul asked me why were they congratulating her? What application? I said I would find out.

I saw Sujata took the medicines from the window and was about to leave. Out of curiosity I rushed to her and said,

'*Namaste Ji*' (Greetings)

'*Namaste*' she replied

'*aap bura na mane to ek baat pooch sakta hu aapse?*' (Would you mind if I ask you a question?)

'*Ji kahiye*' (Yes, please ask)

'What were they congratulating you for?'

'Actually, my application has been approved. I am HIV positive and Government gives money to poor people who are HIV infected so that they can take healthy food and fight this disease. So, from next month onwards I will be getting money directly in my Jan Dhan Bank Account'

'Oh! That's great! Congratulations!'

'Thank you, do you want to apply too?'

'no no ! NO! I am not HIV infected and I am not poor too by God's grace' I'm here with some one and saw everybody was congratulating you, that is why I asked.

'Oh ok'

'I am not sure I should ask you the question that how you did you get infected and how is life treating you now'

'It's ok, you can ask'; Now what's left in the life to hide'

Saying this, Sujata sat down on the chair nearby and took out the water bottle from her bag and started drinking water. Sitting on the chair next to her, I said that I love to hear inspirational and courageous stories of people.

'arey bhaiya, hamari kahani se koi kya seekhega; dukh dard aur sangharsh hi hai, hamari kahani ka saar'

('Hey brother, what will anyone learn from my story; Sorrow, pain and struggle is the essence of my life)

I was listening.

'I am basically from one of the villages in Bihar' I was raped in a state of unconsciousness after getting intoxicant in my food'

'WHAT!!!'

'Yes'

I just went on looking at her face in utter shock. She was telling such a scary incident of her life so easily.

'Haa, mujhe nahi pata ki wo kon log the, koi saboot nahi tha, bahut mushkil se FIR bhi karwayi, lekin saheb, gareeb ko insaaf kab aur kaha milta hai', Bihar ka wo daur, bhulaye nahi bhulta'

(Yes, I didn't know who they were, there was no proof of their identity, even got an FIR done with great difficulty, but sir, when and where does the poor get the justice? That era of Bihar state is unforgettable)

Yet again I could not understand how to react. Sujata continued after reading my face expressions.

'*Ab gaanv mein to maa aur 2 chote bhai behan ke sath rehna mushkil ho raha tha . isiliye babu, hum log shehar me aa gaye*'

(Now it was getting difficult to live in the village with mother and 2 younger brother and sister. That's why we moved to the city)

'*yaha beemar rehne lage, doctor ne HIV test ke liye bataya to Positive nikla*'

(I started getting sick here, when the doctor suggested for an HIV test, it turned out to be positive)

'*Ab mujhe hi maa aur dono bhai behan ko sambhalna hai, beemari ke aage jhuk kar to nahi baith sakte*'

(Now I have to take care of mother and both siblings. You cannot sit by bowing before the disease)

'*haa sahi keh rahi hai aap, aapke bhai behan padhte hai?*'

(Yes, you are right, do your siblings' study?)

'*Haa, sarkari school me*' (yes, in a government school)

'*main kapde ki factory me silayi ka kaam karti hu, wahi se hi paisa aata hai. Lekin ab Sarkar se paise milenge to aur madad ho jayegi*'

('I work in a textile factory, that's where the income comes from. But now if we get money from the government then that would add to the income)

'*haa ye to haai*' (Yes, that's correct), I agreed

'*agar main svasth rahoongee tabhee to parivaar ki zimmedari majabootee se utha paoongee*'

(If I remain healthy then only, I will be able to take the responsibility of the family firmly)

'*Sujata ji, Aapko mera salam hai, aap bahut bahadur hai, aapki kahani un sabhi mahilaon ko prerit karegi jo Zindagi me haa maan kar baith jati hai. Sach me aap hero hai*'

(Sujata Ma'am, I salute you; you are very brave, your story will inspire all those women who give up in their life easily)

'ha ha ha, are saheb, bus yahi Zindagi hai, wo gana suna hai samjhauta ghamo se kar lo' ha ha ha chalo main chalti hu, factory ka time ho gaya'

('Ha ha ha, hey sir, this is just life, have you heard that song 'settle with sorrow' ha ha ha, let me go, it's factory time)

She smiled and left. Sometimes it seems that how people move ahead by making sorrow their companion and learn to be happy. They start **focusing on living instead of fighting**. That day Sujata's story kept running in my mind.

• • •

CHAPTER XI

That's We Call As True Love Story – Geetika & Snehil's Story

You must have heard a lot love stories. There are millions of books, poems/quotes and films that are written and made on true love stories.

What comes to your mind when you think of a love story? A beautiful girl, Handsome guy, flowers, horses, heart shaped balloons, romantic songs, beautiful valleys, chocolates, gifts etc.

Can you imagine, I could find one love story in the hospital itself? In real life?

Yes, Snehil and Geetika's Love story. When Snehil narrated his story to me, tears rolled down my eyes. On that day a living example of true love came to the fore in the form of Snehil and Geetika.

'Friend, you come with me, you come for me, but you spend all the time talking to people? what do you talk to them?' ~ asked the dashing Rahul

'My dear Friend, you take medicine, you meet with the counsellor and then the doctor, in the midst of all this, whatever the time I get, I listen to their stories. I may write a book that will inspire other people'~ I smiled and adjusted my mask

'Okay my writer friend' he smiled too.

Hmmm so I was looking here and there and then I saw a couple. A man was asking a lady to sit down, and he would see that hospital staff has come or not. He passed the water bottle to her.

From their behaviour it seemed that they were husband and wife. The man was standing in the queue for his wife. When her turn came, lady rushed to the queue and man sat to same chair she was sitting earlier.

I was noticing all of this and don't know why I got judgmental and started thinking that surely the poor lady must have been infected because of this man. And I wanted to confirm this.

Although I have no right to enter into someone's personal life, but I have not been able to resist. The earlier 2 stories were quite courageous and inspiring.

'Hi'

'Hello'

'Can I sit here?'

'Yes, sure'

'My name is Rajan and I am here for my friend'

'Oh! My name is Snehil and I am with my wife'

'Nice meeting you Snehil'

'Same here'

How to ask; What to ask? What if he feels bad? Just a flurry of questions was going on and on in my mind.

'Are you also Positive?' Snehil asked

'No, No, just accompanying my friend'

'okay'

'And what about you...Are you positive too?'

'No, today was my wife's medicine day, therefore I'm accompanying her'

'Oh Ok' In General, wives got this infection from their husbands as per my knowledge...but here'? I said this in the quick flow and regretted later

'Excuse Me!'

'I am so sorry, Sir, please don't mind, I just wanted to know how she got this...Sorry'

'But why do you want to know?'

'Oh, actually I would like to write a book on some inspirational stories; thought you too might become inspiration for someone'

'Sorry, not interested, thank you'

His wife came out from the counsellor room, and he ran towards her. I felt very embarrassed and started looking into Instagram reels with my Bluetooth in my ears.

Suddenly someone touched my shoulder and called me. I looked up, Snehil and his wife were standing there. I was terrified and stood up.

'Hi....'

'Hello'

'So Snehil told me that you want to know our story and will publish in some book?' ~ asked confident Geetika

'Oh Yes, I am planning to.... I am working on the same'

'That's a great idea'

'I discussed with Snehil and we are ready'

'Oh great!! Thank You So much'

'Can we go to the private cafeteria outside'? ~ suggested Snehil

'Okay' I said 'let me send a message to my friend'

Rahul would take time; he was yet to meet counsellor and doctor and then he would stand in the queue for medicine. I sent him the message that I was going to the cafeteria outside.

'So, from where we should start' Geetika asked Snehil

'Ha ha your wish' Snehil replied

'Well, Snehil and I were in the same college' he was my best friend at that time.

'Yeah, a friend who used to love her a lot, but madam friend zoned me'

'But you never expressed your feelings to me'

'I was afraid of losing you'

'awww I am getting goosebumps' ~ I interrupted innocently

'So how did you guys finally become the couple from just friends' ~ I asked in curiously

'Close friends' both corrected me together

'Oh ya ya'

'Snehil was my close friend, but I used to love somebody else'

'Wait What!!!' I asked shockingly

'Yes, there was a dude name Manav, who she did not even love but marry too'

'What are you talking!!' I was in absolute shock

'Ha ha, wait for the twist Rajan' ~ Chuckled Geetika

'Then What happened'~ I asked like an inquisitive child who is listening a story from his grandmother

'Yes, Manav and I got married; It was going well until I got to know his secrets': Geetika continued

'Meanwhile I was completely devastated, you can think of a film hero in a bar thinking of his girlfriend who betrayed him' ~ laughed Snehil

'Yeah, but I didn't betray you' ~ She defended herself

'So, what secrets you got to know' ~ I intervened, as I wanted story to continue as Rahul could have come at any point of time

'Secrets about his previous girlfriends, about his sex affairs; I got to know from a girl that Manav was a sex addict'

'Oh my god!' ~ I expressed my shock

'Yes, and then I contacted Snehil and told him all the story'

'The day she called me, I felt very happy to see her name on my cell phone, but she sounded very upset; I met her and then got the whole story'

'We gathered more proofs against him; I told my family and finally filed for divorce'

'That would be a very heart-breaking moment' I said

'Heartbroken as well as that moment I was filled with anger and regret'

Snehil put his hand on Geetika's shoulder

'It took her over one year to get out of that situation' ~ said Snehil

'He was there with me in every situation and then suddenly one day I proposed him when we were with other friends' ~ smiled Geetika taking Snehil's hand in her hand

That was the moment; they were looking into each other eyes and I was feeling like I am watching a romantic movie LIVE.

'Then we got married and here we are' ~ said Geetika

'But how come here? How did the second villain HIV come to your life'? ~ I asked

'It was the shadow of the nightmare we thought we had got rid of' ~ answered Snehil

'Actually, Manav was a sex addict which I was unaware of; I had not gone through any test before marriage and even after divorce'

'And then we got married; It did not come to our notice that we should get tested'

'I started running a small business after my divorce, and I don't want child as of now. My business in new and therefore I want to give my full energy and time to it' ~ explained Geetika

'Therefore, I and Snehil decided to go with Kid thing later. Before divorce I was helping my father in law in his family business. Manav never used protection, and I used to take pills' ~ she added

'But I am the person who is against pills/tablets, as this can damage lever and damage body inside. Therefore, I always use protection and fortunately that protection saved me' ~Snehil

'When I got tested and results came positive, I was filled with guilt that because of me Snehil might have got this. But his test results came negative.' ~ Geetika

'Don't mind Snehil, but what was your reaction when you got to know that Geetika is HIV' ~ I asked

'I was sad, shocked and but at that time I controlled myself and thought what if I were in the place of Geetika. I got all my answers. I love her. She loves me. And we are and will be together in every moment of life, be it happy or sad. And that's the Oath we both took while getting married' ~ smiled Snehil (he was holding her hand)

I was totally mesmerized by the words he said

'I am lucky to have a husband and a friend like Snehil in my life. The best thing God gave me in my life is Snehil' ~ She kissed on his hand

'This is so wonderful, romantic and beautiful. God bless you both, this story to me is the best true love story I have ever heard. You both look great together'~ emotional me with teary eyes

'Ha ha don't cry man' ~ Snehil

'So what about Manav?'

'I was cursing him to the core, then Snehil said that for humanity sake, we should meet Manav and tell him so that he can get himself tested and start the treatment as soon as possible'

'So kind of you Snehil...*aap jaise insan to bhagwan ne banana hi band kar diye ab*' (God has stopped creating people like you, now) ~ I said

'I totally agree with you Rajan' ~ Nodded Geetika

'Ha ha Come on ...enough...so that's our story. I hope you got what you want. I am not sure what inspiration people will get from this though' ~Snehil

'Yes, yes. Now that's we call as true love story and I am sure today's era love birds would inspire from this and would get to know what true love is' ~ I stood up, shook hands; exchanged digits quickly as I saw Rahul entering the cafeteria.

'All the best for your book'

'Thank You and I am very grateful that you guys trusted me. I won't let you down...bye bye'

I caught Rahul at the entrance.

'Bro, they are asking to get a test done from a private lab, they don't do it here'

'Ok will see to it'

'Who were you sitting with?'

'New friends'

'What!!' new friends ? So what will happen to me, now you will forget me Rajan? , Rahul said jokingly

'*Chal na yaar*' (Come on buddy), we 're getting late'

• • •

CHAPTER XII

From Sinner To Saint! – Shreya's Story

'Oh F***!'

'What happened?'

'Look at the girl in the glass cabin with counsellor'

'Who is she?'

'Shreya'

'You mean se......'

'Yeah! Sexy Shreya'

'Oh my god! Oh my god!! What is she doing here?'

'I think she is positive too'

'How are you so sure that she is Shreya? Her face is totally covered, she is wearing glasses too, even her arms are covered and moreover she is in Indian suit'

'Oh! come on...been there, done that;

'What do you mean by that;

'Seriously!!'

'Yeah; Rahul boasted

'f***, and you never told me'

'You were out of town and then I completely forgot.' Now please figure this out how come she is here'

Shreya was one of the beautiful and sexy girls in the college. You just name the latest brand and she has it. She was rich too but her group of friends was not good. Late night parties, low attendance in college and lacking in study. She was seen dropping by and picking up from college in luxurious big cars with different guys.

While Rahul was hiding here and there, I chased Shreya to the parking.

'Hey Shreya'

She looked at me while opening the car door

'Who is this and Sorry I am not Shreya'

'I am...

'You can make fool of him but not me Shreya' Rahul's voice came from behind

'Rahul.... You!'

I was feeling like I am watching some Indian Daily Soap/ Serial with me turning back to Rahul thrice with background sound.

And in the next 15 minutes we three were sitting in a bar nearby.

Let me tell you what happened in those 15 minutes. On the way to bar which Shreya decided to go, both filled me in with what happened in the past.

Shreya's father was very upset when she was caught in the police raid at a bar which was serving liquor to minors. He was so upset that he blocked her all credit/debit cards and she was literally penniless. LOL.

But Shreya was addicted to going parties with her friends. Her friends were also rich. But no matter how rich your friends are, they also support you only for a time. Till when would even those rich friends lend to Shreya? So one damn day, her friend made her meet a guy who used to bring her clients. And in return he used to keep some commission.

'Wait a minute'

'Paid Sex!! Really!?!?'

'Yes'

'I was so frustrated and I didn't have any money to survive'

'But you could have done some part-time job to earn money...BUT WHY this??'

'I thought my father would not like me to do such a small job'

'Oh! Come on Shreya at least 'now' you can be honest, please' ~ Rahul slammed Shreya

'Okay Okay!! I didn't want to do any job, going this way was easier to earn money and live your life the way you wanted to.

I know this was the biggest mistake of my life and I learned the hard way, However, I own and accept my mistakes and can't just keep on cribbing about it.'

'Oh god!! And how come this HIV'?

'At a First, I used to get only one client in a week, as I was very uncomfortable doing that, but then I started getting good money, clients increased, two in a week, and then every day one. And I guess that's how I got that'

'I can never imagine you doing all this'

'When I did for the first time, I could not see myself in the mirror. But when habits become addictions, it becomes very difficult to get rid of them. If you get 5 -10,000 rupees in just one hour, then greed makes your mind its home'

'True'

'So, this is how you became a slut'

'SHUT UP Rahul' I scolded Rahul

I wanted to ask Rahul that how come he knew all about Shreya.

So here ends 15 minutes. After sipping from the glass of wine in a bar, Rahul started his part of the story with Shreya.

'One fine night, Shreya was waiting for her cab on the road, outside a bar and I was also going the same way, I saw her and asked if she needed lift'

'I was drunk and could not go home and my friend was not picking her phone. Therefore, Rahul took me into his gym' ~added Shreya

'There we spent the night and she left in the morning' Rahul concluded

'Oh ! So that's the meaning of 'been there done that'? I asked

Rahul gave a witty smile. Shreya smiled too.

'So, is it possible that, Shreya infected Rahul?'~I asked

'Quite possible' Rahul said 'but I don't blame Shreya for this alone' I also made out with lots of girls without protection....so anything can be possible'

'See Rajan, we both have done mistakes and are repenting for them. But we both cannot sit back for years because of a setback'

'Oh really!! Your friend Rahul was going for suicide after knowing that he is positive'

'Fuck no!!'

'Yeah, this is true Shreya, but then I called Rajan, and he saved me'

'Awww'

'So does your family know about this, Shreya?

'Just my mom! The moment she got to know she slapped hard on my face and then started crying. I made her understand that what HIV is, it is not a disease. AIDS is different. Initially she accompanied me here in the hospital, I made her met with the counsellor and some lady from NGO. Now she is cool.'

'I looked at Rahul'

Rahul understood that I also wanted him to tell everything to his mother. But Rahul ignored me.

'I am thinking of joining the NGO and helping people, making them aware of HIV, STDs and other related things.

I am joining their classes too and reading their materials.'

'Oh! that's great, Shreya!

'Yeah, I don't know how much more life is left with me, but whatever I have, I want to invest in community service. I even sold out all my branded things online as I have got nothing out of it but HIV.'

'So, a Slut has become saint now?' Rahul questioned sarcastically

'SHUT UP RAHUL!!' Shreya and me shouted together

Many times in his life, due to difficult situations, a person takes such steps, which are very difficult to take back. Mistakes for which you are ashamed, but life and luck do not forgive you. So what to do in such a situation? Should we either throw away the rest of our lives by stopping at that very point, cursing ourselves in guilt, or by learning from those mistakes, prevent others from committing such mistakes? Or should guide other people who are trapped in this maze try to get out from there? Maybe that's what Shreya wanted to do, which is a right thing to do.

She dropped us back to the hospital parking where Rahul's bike was parked.

'See you Soon...Bye'

• • •

CHAPTER XIII

The Canada Dream Shattered – Sukhvinder's Story

'I was very excited'

'I was on the cloud 9 and feeling like a rock star'

'All cameras were on me, everybody was taking my picture'

'As I entered the hall, my friends started Bhangra'

'You know how these big fat Punjabi weddings are'

'Yes, it was my wedding day, I was getting married to a beautiful NRI girl from Canada'

This is the story of Sukhvinder Singh who I met with Saurabh in a Seminar on HIV awareness in his NGO.

After the Seminar, they organized a luncheon, and there we started talking.

'So Sukhi Wassup! How is the new job treating you?' ~ asked Saurabh to Sukhvinder aka Sukhi

'Sab changa si '(All is well) ~ he laughed and then we both too and I still don't know the reason

'It's a new job, work is lighter, less hectic as compared to previous one' ~ Sukhi added while putting food in his mouth

'Great! And how is your health? Are you taking medicine on time?'

'Yes yes, always'

'So.....aaa....Sukhi ...how did you....aaaa' ~ I jumped in between, wanted to ask a question to Sukhi but could not.

'How did I get this HIV? Hmmm'

'Yes'

'This is the only Positive thing happened in my life' and he started laughing again and Saurabh added his laughter too

'That was arranged marriage, I liked that girl, she is beautiful'

'We went to Goa for our honeymoon, we stayed over one week there. After Goa we visited our relatives in Mumbai...what a city, man !!'

'Those were the happiest days of my life. The happiest because neither such days have come before, nor will such days ever come'

'We came back to our hometown in Punjab. She stayed for one month and then she left for Canada with a promise that she would finish the paperwork as soon as possible to call me there'

'We used to do video call daily'

"Miss you', 'Love you' were the dialogues come after every 2-3 sentences'

'She was trying to get me to Canada as soon as possible with the help of a lawyer there'

'And I was also taking rounds and rounds to the embassy here'

'Then one day I got a call from Embassy and my brother-in-law accompanied me there'

'I was very sure that today I will get the green signal'

'We both were waiting and a representative came to us and said "Sukhvinder, I am sorry, you have failed the medical test. We double checked and found that you are HIV Positive"'

'FU****!!!!!' – In a big shock I said this with my mouth and eyes wide opened

'Yes, at that moment Life really f*****d me hard and I still feel that pain in my a**' ~ Sukhi

'And the most unfortunate part was that this revelation happened in front of his brother-in-law' ~added Saurabh

'I felt that the earth was torn apart and I would get engulfed. In that very feeling, I could not tolerate this and started running out. My brother-in-law got my intentions and he screamed *"koi fado ohnu, aatm hatya karan ja rehya hai"* (someone please catch him, he is going to do suicide). He along with few staff were running after me, the security guards outside caught me. I knew that my brother-in-law was very angry with me and wanted to ask lots of questions. But he didn't as I was traumatized'

'*phir kya hua*' (then what happened) ~ I asked

'*Phir , phir jhumka gira re .....*' (Then earring dropped)' Sukhi laughed out loud.

Saurabh joined him in his laughter and even me could not resist my laughter.

'Then What bro, he drove me to home and we could not say a word to each other on the way back home. I told to my family and he told to his family about all this sh** happened to me. I tried to call my wife; she didn't pick. I got divorce papers, I signed it and here I am'

'Did she get the infection too?' I asked

'I think yes, not sure though, they never told me. Entire family now knows about it. In the beginning I used to feel very embarrassed, I could not even talk eye to eye with anyone. Then I met Saurabh and he revived the confidence I had lost'

Saurabh smiled.

'*When we're confident, we're more likely to move forward with people and opportunities — not back away from them. And if things don't work out at first, confidence helps us try again. It's the opposite when confidence is low*' ~ Saurabh quoted from somewhere.

Sukhvinder is working now in a reputed firm. He lives his life in his own way. He doesn't try to be happy but stays happy. He likes to wear nice clothes and shoes. He loves going to nightclubs and parties. He goes there on weekends and enjoys a lot with his friends.

'When you make sorrows your friends and learn to live with them, then those sorrows do not give you so much pain'

'A person should not get upset thinking about his sorrows again and again. They will keep on coming in your life by changing forms'

'It is now up to you whether you will be frightened by those sorrows or befriend them smartly and find a way to remove them from your life. And if you can't remove them permanently like in my case, then stop being scared from them and keep fighting' ~ explained Sukhi.

• • •

CHAPTER XIV

We're Gays, Burden To All – Sambhav & Nikesh's Story

'Rahul, Isn't he Nikesh?'

'Who Nitesh?'

'Not Nitesh, but Nikesh, he was in our class, who had left college in between all of sudden'

'Oh yeah that loser.... he should not see us I mean me, go and distract him'

'Ok'

Eh, this Nikesh was some weird guy in our college, and used to remain either alone or with some girls. He had never interacted much with boys. I am not being judgemental but seems like he might have inferiority complex in him. He was intelligent though and a top scorer in the tests, also was kind of favourite student of few teachers. Only because of that thing he was known to the class, as a matter of fact to us. He left the college all of sudden and nobody knew why. And to be very honest nobody cares.

'Hey'

'Hey, do we know each other?'

'You're Nikesh, right? We were in same college and same class'

'Oh yeah, you're the guy who used to participate in debates and other cultural activities'

'Yeah, the only nomination from our class'

We both laughed

'So, how come you are here?'

'Now you have seen me standing in the queue for medicine in this department, I can't tell lie to you, but promise me you won't tell anyone'

'No, no, why would I?'

'I'm here to take mine and my partner's medicines'

'Medicines!! You mean you're....!!!.

'Yes, I am HIV positive'

'Oh! Sorry to hear that'

'hmmm'

'Where is she?'

'Who'?

'Your partner'?'

'Sitting there, but he is HE, not SHE'

'Oh, that means you are ....!

'Yes, I am a gay and he is my partner'

Damn! Sometimes I feel like I don't live in this world and am not aware of anything happening here and there. Am I so into me? No, I am not. Confused!?

'Oh Ok! Hi there'

His partner waved me back, staring at us

'His name is Sambhav'

'Is he not keeping well, looking so dull'

'Yeah, his health is deteriorating' he is getting weaker'

'And because of him and to take care of him You left the college?'

'Partially true, but that time he was quiet fit and healthy, later when the symptoms appeared, we got his test done and found that he is infected.

'I was scared like hell, when he asked me to go for the test too. You know that I have never ever failed any test'

'Yeah, and you passed this too'

'Unfortunately, no' I got positive too'

Nikesh was taking medicine from the counter and I got Rahul's text 'hey I'm going to the counsellor to pass the time, please get rid of him soon'

'So, if you're done here, we can go to the cafeteria to have some tea and snacks'

'Let me ask Sambhav, if he feels ok'

'Hey, he is Rajan, we both studied together in college'

'Hi Sambhav'

'Hi there'

'He is giving us a treat in the cafeteria outside'

'Ha ha ha'

'Not a treat, but yeah, we can sit and chit chat, over coffee or tea, only if you are feeling ok.

'Yeah, I am cool, a coffee is something I need too'

'Great then'

I texted Rahul 'going to cafeteria, will text you once I will be free'

'So, Rajan, how come you're here'? asked Sambhav

'Oh, I was with some NGO guy, who is helping me to write a book on some real life based, true inspirational stories'

'Inspiration from HIV infected people?' ~ Nikesh

'Yes, why not! Even your story can become an inspiration to the people from your community'

'How come'

You have been in relationship for quite a long time, after getting into relation, you both got to know that you guys are infected and are still together and taking care of each other' You can see even heterosexual relations are not that strong in today's time, they break up so easily and can't even resist small temperamental issues'

'Yes, you are right. It was not easy for us to live together; our families have abandoned us' ~Sambhav

'Oh really!!' I asked in a big shock

'The moment I was out to them, they were very upset and asked me to take the treatment; Time flew, but they didn't accept me as a gay'

'Same story with me. When I got in relation with Sambhav, I also told my family, my big brother even slapped on my face Infront of my parents. He said, I am a black spot on the family's reputation.'

'That's very unfortunate' I expressed my sympathy

'This bad fortune starts the day we are born'

'Being gay in the society is like a curse. How many taunts, we have to be heard at every stage of life from childhood till growing up?

You cannot live as real you, you cannot tell anything to anyone. What would the family say, how would the society react? Just being afraid of these questions, life goes on listening to insults. Starting with in family then in school, college and even at your workplace. I don't know sometimes I feel being gay is being an abomination. Why God even created us and sent us on this planet, where nobody respects us, nobody accepts us'

'*Shaant Gada Dhari Bheem Shant!!!* (this a popular hindi slang, spoken to calm down a person who is losing his cool) Sambhav tried to calm down Nikesh

'So, do your families know of HIV?'

'Yes, that was the final nail in the coffin of our loving relation with our respective families; the moment they got to know this, they didn't spend a minute to tell us to leave and stay away from them'

'They were afraid that they can also be infected by HIV because of us' we then parted our ways from our families'

'Oh man!! So tragic Love story'

'What about Sambhav's health.?

'Doctor said that there is nothing to panic, take healthy and nutritious diet, do exercise daily, do not miss out on medicines and do not take stress, he will be alright'

'That's a relief. But seriously hats off to both of you for your courage, confidence and companionship. Your love for each other is so strong that even this incurable VIRUS can not break. Even after so many restrictions from the society, listening to so many taunts from people, your loved ones left you, you guys are holding each other's hands firmly. Yes, Nikesh and Sambhav, your story would be a benchmark for true love specially for LGBTQ people'

'Thank You very much for these lovely words. We got to hear such beautiful and encouraging words after a long time and our hearts throbbed with happiness'

'I echo with Sambhav'

'hmm cool!! I gotta go now, that NGO guy is calling me, hey if you don't mind, can I publish your story in my book?'

'Yeah yeah, not sure if we can inspire anybody, but yes we will be happy to see our story in your book'

'Ha ha , sure, I am paying the cheque for the treat, Bye'

'Okays Bye'

• • •

CHAPTER XV

Sailing In The Same Auto - Rizwan's Story

'What the hell!'

'What has happened to it?'

'IT?'

'I mean 'her''

'I don't know, need to see a doctor'

'You mean mechanic'

Rahul growls at me again.

We were talking about his Motorbike. He loves his Bike very much like a Girl Friend. He never calls her 'it' but 'She'. As he rides on 'it'...sorry 'her' (literally).

'Hey we gonna get late for the hospital, today you need to go for blood test again'

'We can't leave her like this'

'Oh, come on Rahul, you can park her as of now, and we can take auto from outside, come on hurry up!'

He literally worked hard to get his dream bike. It's only Rahul and his god know how hard he earned money to get his dream motorcycle.

'Arey bola to tha tumko ki 8 baje pahuch jaunga', tum bhi waha aa jao' ~ Auto Driver was speaking to someone on phone that to reach there at 8, he would reach there too

(I told you before that I would reach there by 8, you should also come there)

Rahul was not in good mood today, he literally slammed auto wale bhaiya, *'Bhaiya, Phone Choro aur Auto chalao dhyan se' kya tumhari dost, thodi der intzaar nahi kar sakti'*

(Brother, Leave the phone and focus on your driving‘ Can't your girlfriend wait for some time?')

'Bhaiya ji, hamari girlfriend nahi hai, biwi hai' humse milne aa rahi hai'

(She isn't my girlfriend, she is my wife, she is coming to meet me) Replied Auto driver

'Arey auto chalao bhaiya' (Drive your auto)

'Calm down Rahul' We can take your Bike to the service station I mean doctor'. Don't worry, I will go with you' I said this while keeping my hand on his shoulder.

In next 20 minutes I was sitting on the bench watching videos on my phone while waiting for Rahul who was in queue to get the entry slip for blood tests.

'That Auto Driver is in the queue too' ~ says the WhatsApp Notification, received from Rahul.

'Oh f***'

'Seems like he has recognized me and he's staring at me'

'What do you want me to do'

'I don't know. What if he lives in the area near by us and tell other people about me'

' He won't, as both of you are sailing in the same boat ...I mean 'riding in the same auto'...LOL!'

'Rajan, really!! Is this the time for these PJ's?

I could not control my laughter. But the situation was really serious. What if he recognizes Rahul and discloses to all the auto drivers (along with maids, labourers and all) in our area and this way Rahul may get exposed.

I saw that Auto driver was taking to Rahul.

'What the HELL!! Rahul is gone now'

I rushed to him.

'Bhaiya ji aap wahi ho na, jo abhi hamare auto me aaye'

(Hey brother, are you the same person who came in my auto just now) ~ Auto driver confronted Rahul

Rahul didn't say a word and he was looking at me. Rahul was wearing mask though.

'Ye meri biwi hai, Bushra and mera naam Rizwan hai'

(She is my wife Bushra and my name is Rizwan)

'Ok bhaiya, aap yaha kaise' I asked

(Okay, how come you 're here?) – I asked

'Arey kaise baat pooch rahe hai aap bhaiya ji, yaha to sab ek hi beemari ke liye hai na. aapko bhi to wahi hogi'

(What are you asking brother, everybody is here for one disease and you might be having the same)

'Nahi nahi bhaiya , mujhe nahi hai'

(No No , I don't have that one) I literally said in disgust.

'Aur yaha khade hone ka matlab hamesha ye nahi hai ki aap bhi grasit hain)

And standing here doesn't always mean that you're infected too. I tried to make him convince.

'sahi keh rahe hai , bhai jaan' Bushra agreed to my point

(You are right)

'Tu chup kar...

haa wo to hai bhai ji , lekin aapka dost kyu line me khada hai?'

(You shut up...(Rizwan to Bushra...)

...that's agreeable but why is your friend standing in the queue?)

'Bhaiya mujhe ek competition me bhag lene liye test karwane hai, yaha test free hote hai to isiliye' Rahul jumped in quickly to answer Rizwan

(To participate in a competition, I need to go for these tests and here the tests are free of cost, therefore)

'Haa haa' I said yes in sycophancy

'achha bhaiya'

(Ok Brother)

Seems like he was convinced with Rahul's reply.

But no matter how much you hide the lie, it can't stay hidden for long. That was a big coincidence, that both Rahul and Rizwan got the TB medicines at the same day and at the same time. Yes, they started his tuberculosis prevention medicines that day. The moment Rahul took the medicines from the counter, he was shocked to see the auto driver standing behind him.

'*mujhe to pehle se hi pata tha bhaiya ji, 'ye to bade wala LOL ho gaya'* Rizwan laughed and we both were embarrassed.

(I knew it before brother, this is a LOL moment)

'*Aaiye bhaiya ji, ghar chor du..ghabraiye nahi main kisi ko nahi bataunga*' Rizwan shouted sitting in the auto while we were waiting for the auto on the road.

(Come on brother, let me drop you home, and do not worry, I won't tell anyone)

I looked at Rahul.

'Now the bird has devoured the field already, there's is no need to regret'? Rahul used an apt idiom on the situation

'*Aapko ye sab kaise hua bhaiya;? Kya aapki biwi ko bhi hai?*'

(How did all this happen to you, brother? Does your wife have too?')

Before Rizwan asked us more questions, I turned the table towards him. Rahul was in no mood to talk of *any kind*.

'*Main ek auto driver hoon aur ghar pe hamara kuch packing ka kaam hai, hum miya biwi wo hi karte hain*'

('I am an auto driver and we have some packaging work at home in the morning, we husband and wife do that together')

He told us that he has been driving the auto before marriage as his father was also an auto driver. Because he used to drive the auto in the night, he met lots of transgenders, prostitutes and gays for paid sex. He did with few of them and that to without protection.

'Ab kya batayein saab, sex cheez hi aisi hai, jawani ke din the, control nahi tha, to jo mila pel diya'

('Now what to tell you sir, Sex was like a thing that there was no control in the days of youth, so whatever I got, I screwed them')

Rahul and I were looking at each other, we were about to burst with laughter of awkwardness, but we controlled somehow.

'to bhaiya Bushra ko aapse hua?'

(So, Bushra got infected from you?')

'Bhaiya ab ye HIV ka ek dum se to pata nahi chalta, nikaah ho gaya tha, to ab Bushra bhi dawai leti hai')

('Brother, now this HIV is not known at once, the marriage was done, so now Bushra also takes medicine with me')

I asked Rizwan if he ever regretted his actions. He humbly replied 'Almighty would have punished me for my mistakes, but he punished Bushra too, that's the only sad thing'

'When Bushra came to know about all this, she could have left me, but she said that we have done love marriage and our love cannot be so weak that a tiny virus can break it' Rizwan said it emotionally and with pride.

'yaha left me rok dijiye. Aur haa bhaiyaa....'

(Pull over to the left and brother....)

'haa haa, main kisi se kuch nahi kahunga, aap chinta na kare'

(Yeah, I got it, I won't tell anyone about him, you don't worry)

'Thank You'

'Nice guy'

'Really!!?'

'He said he won't tell anyone, Rahul'

'Not that'

'Then what'

'What if Rizwan had got an infection from Bushra? So, would he have been handling the relationship in the same way as her?? You should have asked this question to him'

'Perhaps not. Perhaps yes. You never know. Remember Snehil and Geetika'

'hmmm'

'What is the inspiration from this story?' Rahul asked in sarcasm. 'coz there was none.

'Not inspiration but a strong message that to control your emotions and energy before they get wasted. It is very important to keep your senses under control.

If you become uncontrollable and you are not able to direct that energy in an apt direction, then you can be wasted. And this wastage will not be confined only to you, but it will also affect your loved ones'.

'Correct'

'From where this duo of Jai and Veeru coming? Rahul's Mom asked from the balcony

'Jogging mom, Rajan is putting on weight'

'F*** off'

• • •

CHAPTER XVI

Moms Are Supernatural

You must have heard of super heroes and supernatural, they have special powers of super hearing, sight, fast healing, sniffing the scent and tracking the person, some do magic too, and they also do multitask at the same time. Sometimes I feel that God has created mothers with special powers and she is the real supernatural.

Rahul's new life was now about to complete two years. I have been accompanying him every time he visits hospital. in his very limited friend circle, I was the only one who knows all about Rahul. But eventually i had to leave the city as I had got the appointment letter for my job. That time Rahul too had established his gymnasium and personal training business very well. During the past one year, on different occasions, I tried to convince Rahul that he should tell his secret to his mother. But he kind of avoided that topic always.

Rahul is a person who needs encouragement and motivation at different intervals in order for him to achieve the target, accomplish the task or to move on with his life positively. The HIV revelation had hammered his mind, heart and soul. He was a completely changed and grown-up man. However, being worried about him, when I discussed the topic of 'telling Mom', he shockingly said 'yes' this time.

'Mom, I want to tell you something'

'Yes, tell me, I have some time before going to the office'

'We can discuss it when you'll come back in the evening'

'No no, I have all the time in the world for you'

'It's a big thing mom, I wanted to tell you but could not gather the courage'

'Oh! is there some girl you want me to meet?' ~ Mom chuckles.

'No Mom! no girl!'

'Oh My god! so a boy? You're gay? ... don't you worry son, I support LGBT, I am not like other moms'

'*Arey mom kya bol rahe ho aap*, I 'm straight' (Mom, what are you saying, I'm straight)

Mom laughed.

'What!!'

'I know your big secret *beta* (son).... You are HIV Positive'

Rahul was literally shocked to hear his secret from her mom, and she said it casually

'How do you know?'

'I am your mother, and mothers know everything. Your changed behaviour, adopting new habits, no parties, no girls, limited friends, always remain serious at home and moreover you started locking your drawers now. What did you think, your mother would not notice all this?'

'So, what are you? Supernatural!?'

'ha ha ...yeah sort of! Maid found a medicine box in your room's trash bin while cleaning, I saw it and researched it on the internet. That way I got to know those were HIV medicines'

'Oh!' My bad, I was in hurry and accidentally threw that empty box in the bin'

'That's not the thing, but son this is serious, you are educated and how come you became HIV Positive'

'Mom, I gotta go now' Rahul was feeling embarassed

'I can understand what you must have been through, but baby, I am your mother, you could have shared this with me'

'Mom, I was ashamed of myself. I even... thought of attempting suicide too. But I called Rajan and he saved me, helped me to sail through that difficult time'

'Thank god!! Rajan is a good guy, god bless him'

Rahul was telling me his conversation with his mom and suddenly he stopped.

I asked 'what else mom said about me'

'Nothing, *bus itna hi bola*' (that's what she said) and then he laughed.

'*Bata na yaar, Aunty ne kya kaha*' (tell me friend, what did Aunty say)

'*Kaisa mara ja raha hai tareef sunne ko*' (look how you're dying to listen to your praise)

'F'get it'

'Mom said such friends are found only by good luck'

'Yay!! You're the lucky one then

'It seemed difficult to tell mom, it turned out to be as easy. It feels like a heavy load has been taken off from my heart and mind and I'm free now'

'I understand, so now when I am gone, you have someone who can take care of you, and you can share things'

'Yeah'

'But how did that conversation end?'

'Mom said she researched about this and read about this, also she visited a counsellor too by her own, and she is now clear on her doubts about HIV'

'That's cool!'

We both smiled and that's how the day ended happily, freely and accomplished.

• • •

The World In 2030

In one of the seminars organized by Saurabh's NGO, they were explaining the UNICEF report on HIV and AIDS. Out of curiosity I studied that report too and found that **sub-Saharan Africa is the epicentre of HIV and AIDS.** According to the UNICEF's data and research, 2.78 million children and adolescents were living with HIV, nearly 88 per cent of them in sub-Saharan Africa.

In 2020, of the estimated 38.0 million people living with HIV worldwide, an estimated 2.78 million were children and adolescents aged 0–19 years. In the same year, 300,000 children and adolescents were newly infected with HIV and 120,000 children and adolescents died of AIDS-related causes. Every day in 2020, approximately 850 children aged 0–19 years became newly infected with HIV and approximately 330 children aged 0–19 years died from AIDS–related causes, mostly because of inadequate access to high-quality HIV prevention, care and treatment services.

The World in 2030

Even with success, a large population of children and adolescents living with HIV will need access to services well beyond 2030. Data says

- 1.9 million children and adolescents are projected to be living with HIV
- 270,000 children and adolescents are projected to become newly infected with the virus annually
- 56,000 children and adolescents are projected to die from AIDS-related causes annually
- 2.0 million new HIV infections could be averted

between 2018 and 2030 if global goals are met − 1.5 million of these would be averted among adolescents

UNICEF's Prediction - A staggering 360,000 adolescents are projected to die of AIDS-related diseases between 2018 and 2030 without additional investment in HIV prevention, testing and treatment programs
Source: UNICEF.org
Monitoring the situation of children and women

• • •

Accept, Learn & Move On

If someone gets courage after reading all these stories and will not be afraid of the troubles but fight against them firmly, then it will be worthwhile for me to write this book. Those on whom these troubles have come, who have progressed in life after fighting those troubles and those people who fight with different types of troubles every day, only those people can give courage to others.

Whether that 18-year-old '**Ajay**', whose fate HIV had already written even before he was born or that 45-year-old **Sujata** who doesn't even know that who did the heinous thing to her and how she got HIV, or whether it is **Sukhwinder** who got to know that he is HIV positive in fornt of his in-laws or that **Snehil** who loves his wife **Geetika** even after knowing that she got HIV from her ex-husband, everyone has found solutions to their problems in their own way.

And yes, **Rahul**, the whole life is lying in front of him, who has accepted his mistakes and learning from them. He believes that now he has to live not with problems but with solutions. He has become more responsible now and started taking life seriously. He now knows what his life is worth of and he doesn't want to waste even one second of it.

The meaning of life is not to stop, but just keep moving. Death is inevitable, therefore do not stop living, try to live every moment of it to the fullest. Do not just sit back and give up because with your blood, a virus is flowing in your veins too. You can't destroy it but you can control it and live a healthy life for long. Being infected with HIV does not end life, does not end aspirations, does not erase the desire to get something and to become something in life.

'जातस्य हि ध्रुवो मृत्युर्ध्रुवं जन्म मृतस्य च ।
तस्मादपरिहार्येऽर्थे न त्वं शोचतिमर्हसि ।।२७।।'

jātasya hi dhruvo mṛtyurdhruvaṃ janma mṛtasya ch
tasmādaparihārye'rthe na tvaṃ śocitumarhasi ~ The
Bhagavad Gita, Chapter 2 – Verse 27

Meaning - Indeed, certain is death for the born, and certain is birth for the dead; therefore, over the inevitable, you should not grieve, you should not lament.

• • •